I0760880

Everyday Pocket Poetry

LOANN TWEDT RN, BS, MA, DE

Everyday Pocket Poetry

ISBN
978-1-957378-25-1 (Hardcover)
978-1-956161-66-3 (Paperback)
978-1-956161-65-6 (eBook)

THE AUTHOR AND THE BOOK

LoAnn Twedt is a 75-year-old woman who is a widow, a mother, a grandmother, and a great grandmother. She was raised on a farm in Minnesota, a rural girl. She was educated as a nurse, a business woman, a counselor, an academic psychologist and writer. Her first self publication was a newsletter that was distributed to doctors, nurses, friends and acquaintances. It was called *"Physician's Weekly"* that was published by a division of her company, PostScripts Publishing, under the umbrella of LifeChange Industries, a Minnesota based company. Several poems and some introductory statements are taken from her newsletter. A collection of poems were written during the time she published the Physician's Weekly. Her desire is to continue writing more poetry and short essays in collections for books. Two of her poems have been published in coffee table books; *"Gone Fishin'"*, *"Traveling Home"* and *"On the Beach"* won an Editor's Award in contest. You will find these poems in this book.

The book is made up of poems on her everyday life and the events that happened or crossed her path on any given day, - Thus the name, *"Everyday Pocket Poetry"*. It is her desire to have a book small to fit in a pocket or purse for use with groups, in break time entertainment and as a carry-along for caregivers to read for those who cannot read for themselves. The objective in writing these poems was to uplift the readers, make them think, encourage them, and provide laughter and pleasure.

Poems are often written with music playing, usually children's songs, because they lend an air of lightness and fun to the process. Mrs. Twedt volunteers time with piano playing and conducting reminiscence groups for facilities such as assisted living homes, nursing homes, Alzheimer and dementia groups and senior dining groups. She routinely looks after her neighbors and helps with any healthcare needs they may have. Nurses never retire but often continue caring for people with volunteer services.

Mrs. Twedt's hope is that readers will enjoy the book and use it as tool to improve the lives of others. With that said, enjoy your time with her.

I must give a special thank you to my daughter, Sarah, for her illustration of the book cover. Without my children, Sarah and Jason, many of these poems would not have been written. Thank you kids!

TABLE OF CONTENTS

Everyday Poetry

ALONG THE BEACH

(Editor's Award)
LoAnn Twedt © 1999

Along the beach the empty
Shells lay strewn about
As though looking for a tomorrow
That will never come.
I walk among them,
Sand gushing between my toes,
Telling me that time has no
Hold on me here.
The ocean breeze gently blows
The wisps of my curly hair,
As though it longs to comb
This mane into something more
In tune with the song of sea gulls.
I stoop to grasp a shell
That whistles with a mellow, lusty drone
To the ghosts that walk the waters.
And, in the distance, a gull
Cries, circles, dives and one
Creature of the sea is no more.

THE CEDAR TREE

It stands alone
Against the winds of time.
Its roots so firmly planted that,
No matter how hard the wind blows,
It will stand firm in its resolve
To remain a living thing.

LOOKING IN THE MIRROR

LoAnn Twedt © 2002

How many of us can honestly say
We enjoy looking in the mirror?
The shape of "things" on any given day
Could certainly be clearer.
My head's too small and butt too big,
Your leg's too short and chest too flat.
Aghast and shocked, we wither like a fig,
And our ego goes Ker-splat!
To help us out of such a slump,
It's worthwhile to recall,
Our Lord doesn't think us junk,
And, with His help, we can love it all.

PONDERING

LoAnn Twedt © 2002

I sat before the mirror
Wondering, "Who was that
Looking back at me?"
I thought, "That girl sure looks sad."
I could see in her face, her eyes
A hint of fear that, perhaps, her life
Would not be real again.
It all just seemed so far away.
Will she laugh again?
Run barefoot through the grass?
Will she lie looking at clouds
On a warm summer day?
Or will she stay before the mirror
Gazing at eyes that don't shine
With tears that won't come?

CHILD'S PLAY

LoAnn Twedt © 2002

It came to mind one summer day,
That I have no voice in what to say,
When summer sun turns to fire.

Though water in my glass is wet,
Without a move, I copiously sweat,
When summer is so warm.

Down my face, back and legs
A stream runs in rivulet dregs.
Down and down into my sandals.

The children seem to run and play
Even when asked inside to stay.
To keep them safe from heat.

Oh, for the energy of youth,
That of kicking heels and blatant truth.
Where did the energy go?

If I were but a prepubescent,
I'd scoot about without habiliments.
Free from stricture in the open air,
With mane a-flyin' and cheeks so bare.

FRIENDS

LoAnn Twedt © 1999

Friends are like a summer breeze,
That cools a sweaty brow.
Friends are like the shade of trees,
That stretch with bended bow.

Friends will last eternally,
When Jesus Christ they love.
Friends will strong and faithful be,
With guidance from above.

Friends can sit and coffee sip,
With not a spoken word.
Friends can speak up quite a bit,
And never once be heard.

Friends do care and give support,
When times get, "oh so low";
And friends do sent their spirit,
Where others dare not go.

LIMMERICS AND HAIKU?

LoAnn Twedt © 2001

SUMMERTIME

T'is almost time for summer run
And sitting in the sun.
So grab a beer and make it clear.
You're here to have some fun.

MAN

Man can think as many,
Produce as a few,
But be as only one.

ALL OF ME

Although I seem fragmented,
Like there are more of me.
To know the few
Brings laughter true,
And slapping of the knee.

WRITER'S BLOCK

LoAnn Twedt ©

What to do with aching head?
When seems you should have gone to bed.

And here you sit with bleary eyes,
With aching back you can't disguise.

Today is done with weary dread,
"I know my limit", you firmly said.

But before the mouse has time to play,
You'll see the break of another day.

THE SWIMMER

LoAnn Twedt © 1999

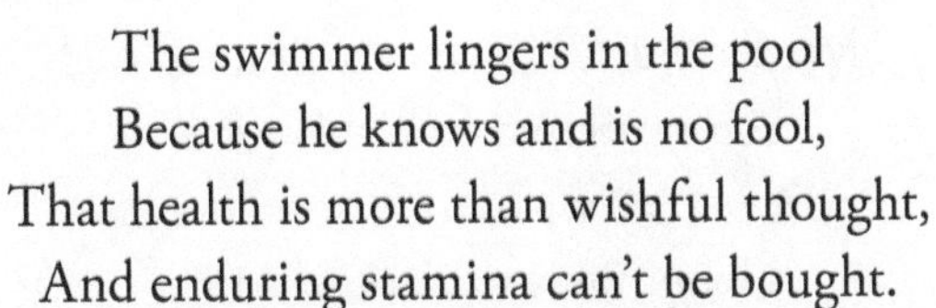

The swimmer lingers in the pool
Because he knows and is no fool,
That health is more than wishful thought,
And enduring stamina can't be bought.

The water's just like mother's womb,
With quiet peace and private room.
What shape you start in is no matter,
What counts is making a big splatter.

For what is resting in your heart,
Is more that outer shells impart.
Friendships found so strong and true,
Are waiting there for me and you.

MY GRANDPA'S HANDS

LoAnn Twedt © 2000

My Grandpa's hands are tan and big
And callused from his work.
They play with mine and do a jig
Upon his sweat-stained shirt.

My Grandpa's fingers are so tall,
But our fingers still entwine.
My fingers, they are very small,
And to him they feel so fine.

And while he taps each finger tip,
He hums a little tune.
His eyes are full of love and zip,
He stops just way too soon.
(For Sarah)

THE ARTIST

LoAnn Twedt © 2001

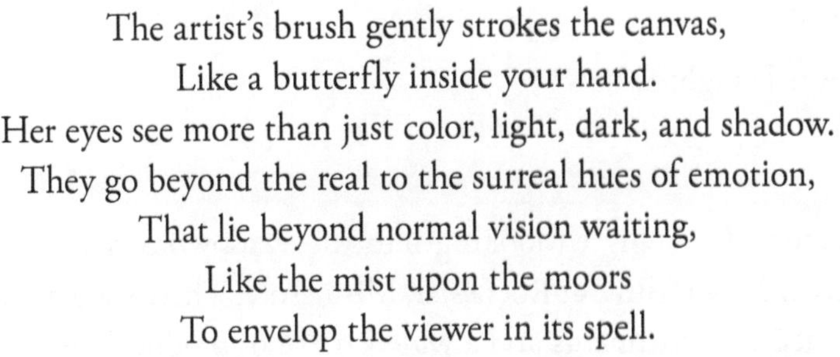

The artist's brush gently strokes the canvas,
Like a butterfly inside your hand.
Her eyes see more than just color, light, dark, and shadow.
They go beyond the real to the surreal hues of emotion,
That lie beyond normal vision waiting,
Like the mist upon the moors
To envelop the viewer in its spell.

Oh, what do you see, Miss, in your mind's eye?
"The colors of life and hues of pain,
The imprint of music on the soul,
And the melody of a bird's song,
As it sends streamers of sound to listening ears.
But most of all, I see my own reflection
Looking back at me from my shadowbox of life."

(Happy Birthday, Sarah)

My Dear Daughter,

In memory, I saw myself looking into the shadowbox displays in the tunnels of Mayo Clinic at Rochester, Minnesota. There were diamonds, hats, musical instruments and a wide variety of products displayed for sale in those shadowboxes. I thought of you and your mind's eye and how you would possibly see those items in a different and more personal perspective, as I think, I actually saw them too.

My earnest wish for you is that you continue to visualize and absorb the things you see and allow them to create shadowbox displays in your mind's eye so they can be transferred to canvas for all to enjoy.

Love dear and true,

Mom

SATISFACTION

LoAnn Twedt © 1999

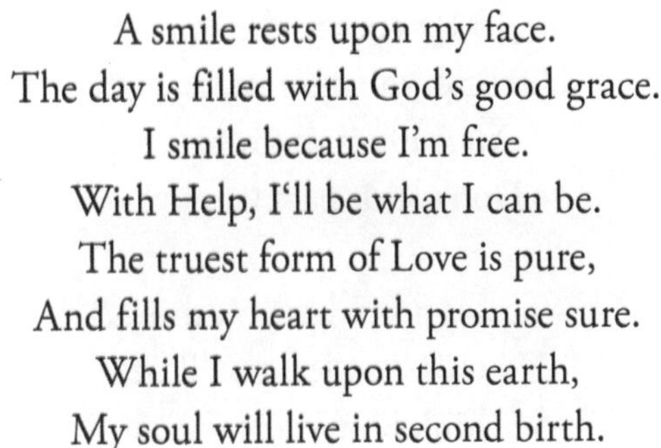

A smile rests upon my face.
The day is filled with God's good grace.
I smile because I'm free.
With Help, I'll be what I can be.
The truest form of Love is pure,
And fills my heart with promise sure.
While I walk upon this earth,
My soul will live in second birth.

WHO ARE YOU?

LoAnn Twedt © 2004

To fly among the stars
Or climb the mountains high
Your life is up to you.
Don't let it pass you by!

You are just what you think,
No more, no less you'll be.
So think how you can soar
Beyond what you can see.

Your dreams are seeds from God.
Your talents tell you true
The path that you can take,
So to yourself be true.

THE LITTLE WHITE RABBIT AND THE LITTLE BROWN PUP

LoAnn Twedt © 2002

The little white rabbit and the little brown pup
Are helping me so I grow up.
I'm still a little child, you see,
Who fears the dark and the Jiggle-dee dee.

These two good friends are always there,
When I go to bed up the stair.
They lay by me all through the night,
True companions in any plight.

In the morning, when I awake,
There they are! For goodness sake!
They've been on watch all the time
That I've been sleeping so sublime.

I greet them each with happy glee,
Because they're faithfully there for me.
Sometimes when Mom and Dad aren't there,
It's ok to have them close, this pair.

Such a comfort, in the night,
Helps banish all the gloom and fright.
I can dream without a care
When fast asleep with hound and hare.

I DON'T KNOW; THE ONLY ANSWER

LoAnn Twedt © 2001

Off I go to Ephrata,
E-Freight-A that is.
Looking for my Dad.

Will I find him? I don't know,
Or will I find his fragrance, left behind
Of a rich life with the flower of youth
And decay of old age?

The psychic says there is danger
Here in Ephrata
As she lights her candles.

Is there danger in Ephrata? I don't know.
How will I know?
When it sneaks on cat paws from behind
To wrap its claws about my frame,
And pull me to the ground?

My friend fears for my life,
As she sits and prays for my care
With all the love she holds.

Do I feel her fear? I don't know.
Perhaps, because she is my friend
And our souls stretch, longing for touch,
When we are far apart.
I call her. She is happy and comforted.

In Ephrata I find friends
Who call their relatives
To join my search for Dad.

Will they help? I don't know.
Their intentions are wonderful,
But each one leads in a different direction.
I am one and can take only one course.
The phonebook.

James Wilson lies in wait
To talk to me.
He is my Dad.

Will he talk to me? I don't know.
Tomorrow I call to find him.
Where I go from here only God knows.
The trail seems to go on forever,
And I am finite.
Where I go is determined
By the willingness of others
To share with me their lives.

Will they share? I don't know.
It seems so as I listen
To sympathetic voices on the phone.
But how much did they share?
And is it enough?

I don't know.
And never will,
Until I find my Dad.

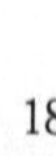

THE WINDOWS OF MY SOUL

LoAnn Twedt © 2001

From the windows of my soul,
The view is part of me.
The scenes are sometimes troubled,
And sometimes filled with glee.
Stories roll before my eyes,
And characters are strange.
Before I have a chance to talk,
These characters all change.
At such a pace, it's really hard to know
Why each story can puzzle me so.
It seems that someone has control
Of all those silly scenes.
And I can't understand at all
What half of this all means.
Peering through those windows
Each night wondering what I'll see
I firmly have to keep in mind,
That I'm really seeing me!

LABORERS

In health care, the most important component of facility health is the laborer. The different departments of housekeeping, maintenance, nursing, social services and administration all play an important part of making the facility run properly and well in the care of patients.

The most important person in the nursing facility is the patient. The nursing staff works daily to make certain the patient is first for care and understanding. The process begins with the Director of Nurses. Clerical nursing staff coordinates patient care, physical therapy, social services, kitchen services and housekeeping. Maintenance is informed about what is needed in facility function to enhance the residents' health and care. However, the nursing assistant is the backbone of care. They are the people who provide "hands-on" care to individuals who need help in all facets of life. Their job is the one that requires heavy labor, lifting people and hauling items with which most people want nothing to do. Staff nurses and nursing assistants are there with people and their families when they go through difficult times of illness, relationship issues and death to deal with the distress this causes. These are the people that count the most to the patient.

In other businesses and organizations, management directs, trains and guides the workers to perform as they should for the benefit of the customer. The down line is no different than with health care. If management is dysfunctional, so are the workers they direct because chaos comes from the top down. Workers know when management is dysfunctional because it affects their day's work – every day.

The following poems are concerning the worker's plight and the honor that should be bestowed for a job well done.

THE LABORER

LoAnn Twedt © 1999

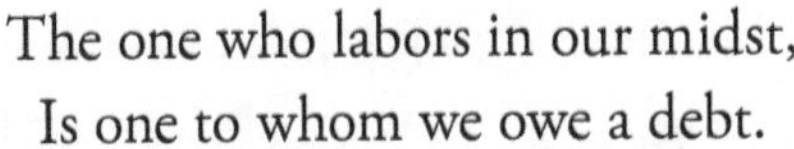

The one who labors in our midst,
Is one to whom we owe a debt.

For that's the one whom God has set
To serve a special purpose yet.

For when his work is finally done,
The Lord will move him to the next;

And we will be the better off,
Because he served us though perplexed.

The Worker's Question

What have you fed your body today?
And what have you fed your soul?

CHAOS

LoAnn Twedt © 1999

This morning I jumped out of bed
With enlightened thoughts inside my head.
Soon the day began to take
A different visage for goodness sake.
Faithful subordinates
Became inordinate.
Our country gent shook his cane.
I thought the place had gone insane!
And then a little voice did start
To well up from inside my heart.
"This day is Mine," He said to me,
Whatever I will ask of thee;
It won't be more than you can bear.
It will not show that I don't care.
For in this day, you will learn,
And for my help you'll surely yearn.
And learn I did, without a doubt;
That chaos I can do without!
This day, years from life were spent.
I now know peace is heaven sent.

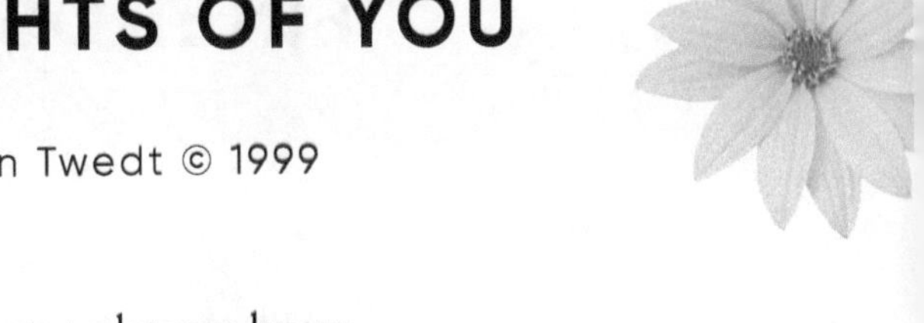

THOUGHTS OF YOU

LoAnn Twedt © 1999

Just a note to let you know
You're thought of every day,
With kindest thoughts and wishes
That God will send your way

It matters little what you may do
That turns the tide of change.
It's who you are and that you are
Although that may seem strange.

For God inside your soul has put
A spirit filled with power.
And His love will guide your hand
From hour onto hour.

Soon your day will be spent
Tending to the needs of all,
And as you rest, remember this
You've answered well His call.
(Poem for health care professionals)

FRIENDSHIP

LoAnn Twedt © 1999

When you feel like this
And your day is not bliss
Remember me and smile.

I will be your friend,
And your day will end
With cheer most undefiled.

PROFOUND LIVING

It has been, since the conception of LifeChange Industries, that the psalmist's words in Psalms 139:13-14 have been the focus of all health educational services extended by the company. " You [God] created my inmost being, You knit me together in my mother's womb, I praise You because I am fearfully and wonderfully made." (NIV Bible, 1995, Zondervan Publishing) The verses convey a profound realization of who we are and what we are worth to the Creator of all life. While we treat the broken limbs, hearts, and spirits of those who seek our services, we can recall their value to God and see in them the reflection of our own faces. (1999)

SEASONS OF THE YEAR

Seasons of the year have often been compared to seasons of our lives. I'm afraid you will not find that in this book. It happens to be fodder for the next book I'm writing. This book contains serious thought provoking descriptions of what happens during the seasons and a little humorous look at our seasonal activities.

JANUARY IS COLD

LoAnn Twedt © 2021

In January the old stay in
And it's a time we just can't win.
Flu and cold season are all about,
Time to bundle up and not go out.

Most of us don't see each other all winter.
In spring we make up all we missed, and friendships don't splinter.
We gather on someone's porch for a long visit,
And winter? We never miss it.

FEBRUARY: TIME FOR LOVE

Even the old know love,
And long for someone to hold.
Like the pair of turtle doves,
February can make us bold.

It's still a time to bundle up,
Even in the house,
A cute little fuzzy pup?
No, better yet, a warm-blooded spouse.

Valentine's Day can bring out the suitor,
Just like when younger.
Bonding, comforting, sharing we don't need a tutor.
But the day is still filled with wonder.

MARCH KITES

In March it is fun to watch the children fly their kites.
Memories abound as the wind takes the kite higher.
We shout and cheer for the child and the wind.
A fire and marsh mellows are great over a hot pyre.

The weather is a bit warmer, and indication spring is coming.
Early flowers peak their heads above ground.
They make us smile, for warmth is around the corner.
We button up our coat and walk about humming.

SPRING FLOWERS

LoAnn Twedt © 2017

Oh, the joy and excitement
Of planting flowers
One can hardly wait
For April's plenty showers.

To put that trowel into the dirt
Is pleasure pure and true.
Visions of beautiful buds
Seem to fly in from the blue.

Showers come and small plants grow.
The heart follows the ebbing tide
Of the growing season's work.
The gardener goes along for the ride.

Blossoms arrive in copious profusion,
The wonder of such beauty glows
Within the breast of those who sow,
And the sun shines down on those who grow.

APRIL SHOWERS BRING MAY FLOWERS

LoAnn Twedt © 2017

In May the flowers bloom and grow
Filling the beds with colorful profusion.
And as if God planned this all through
Mother's Day is here.

It's usually mother that plants
The garden beds and helps them all to grow.
She grows her children in her womb.
And when the time is here to birth
Another precious jewel is born.

As summer comes, the child grows.
Mother watches with anxious breath,
Her child steeped in play.
She's there to mend the broken heart.

INTELLIGENCE

LoAnn Twedt © 1999
(Physician's Weekly, PostScripts Publishing)

Oh, ye doctors of great wisdom and knowledge,
Remember your mothers and the mother of your children.
Your male children have received 100 percent of their intelligence
From these noble women, and that's the truth.
Check that out!
(Daniel Goleman, 1994, Bantam Books, New York)

SUMMER DAYS

LoAnn Twedt © 2017

In June, the summer sun
Will make the flowers grow.
Tall and straight
Row on row.

The vegetables peak up
And grow with vigor.
Some are early some are late
Oh, dear! The patch must be bigger.

Fruit hangs from the trees.
Plump and luxuriante
It grows and grows
Our spirit grows totally exhuberant.

JULY

LoAnn Twedt © 1999

In warm July the clouds fly by,
When chased upon the wind.

Children play and run all day,
With laughter and a grin.

You and I sit nearby,
Pondering where we've been.

LIFE EXPANSION

LoAnn Twedt © 1999
(PostScripts Publishing)

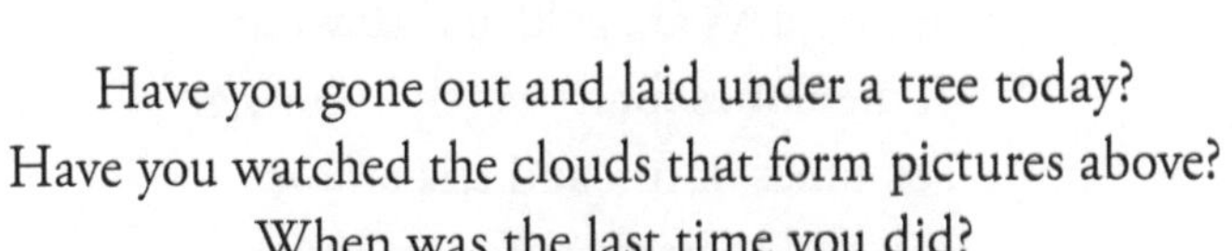

Have you gone out and laid under a tree today?
Have you watched the clouds that form pictures above?
When was the last time you did?

GONE FISHIN'

LoAnn Twedt © 2001

Summer days are gold and flowing,
With memories fond- worth knowing.
For times of fun and relaxation,
Will add to winter time creation.
So how you spend this summer day
Is more than important, in a way.
Memories made in fun and laughter
Will linger on the mind here after.
And fishin's one memory fond
Of Grandpa's pasture fishin' pond.
A walk along the well-worn cow path,
A tin of worms and thought of creek bath
Are just a few of life's small treasures,
That harvest after summer pleasures.
So think about what you might say,
When asked what you might do today.
Instead of mourning what you're wishin'
Get that pole and let's go fishin'!

COWS

LoAnn Twedt © 2021

I've never seen such sweet repose
With ever so much grace.
Cows look at you with great big eyes
And quite a longing face.

Cows graze withing the pasture green
And chew their rich, nutritious cuds.
Tending to their little calves,
That stand close by like flower buds.

What do they think about out there,
The wolf or lion, bull or bear?
It seems they think about their calves
Who run about with gust and bubble.

Don't get between the two, or you will be in trouble!

THE MONTH OF AUGUST

LoAnn Twedt © 2017

Late summer brings the smell
Of maturing crops and fruit.
The sun shines bright
Times of storms are gone.

The corn and beans drape the fields
Where you heard them grow,
And sit ripening their
Fruits for harvest.

There are no better smells
For the farmer of crops.
For his work
Is almost done

The smell of hay being bailed
Straw bales going into the mow
Chickens clucking while eating grain
Vegetables being canned.

All is part of August
As the growing season
Begins to slow down
And time for harvest is near.

SEPTEMBER

LoAnn Twedt © 2017

Canning and preserving almost done,
The time is here to pick berries.
Fruit of the vine is now in season.
Work continues as we water bath cherries.

Pick the wild fruit along the ditches.
Bring them home for jams and jellies.
As we work we taste and giggle.
Sweetness fills our little bellies.

Take Lady B for a ride.
The leaves are beginning to turn.
Yellow, red. gold and brown
Colors and sounds softly churn.

Summer is coming to an end
Fall will soon be here.
We sigh as school starts.
School bell rings loud and clear.

OCTOBER

LoAnn Twedt © 2017

It's harvest time.
Dust is in the air.
The farmer and his tractor
Make an impressive pair.

Goldenrod is blooming
Pollen abounds.
Running nose and sneezing
Is going all around.

Keep on working then
For hours upon hours
The farmer's work is never done
Even with great horse power.

But when the grain is in the cribs
And farmer's cows are fed.
Long hours seem to melt away
When he hits his comfy bed.

NOVEMBER

LoAnn Twedt © 2017

November has its own attraction
Color's gone but satisfaction
Fills the day.

Leaves are leaving in heavy number
Raking, sweeping without cumber
Takes the hours one by one.

November days are cool and brisk.
The winds around the shoulders whip.
We know that winter's coming.

FAMILY TIES

LoAnn Twedt © 2003 (For Jason)

Although it seems we're far away,
Our spirits meet in prayer and play.

Close your eyes and see the plain,
Where imaginations come to meet again.

I see you and you see me on this Thanksgiving Day.
To God in heaven, we give our praise and pray.

And while we play in our mind's eye,
The incense of our joy rises to the sky.

THANKSGIVING DAYS

LoAnn Twedt © 2001
Blessings and hope for much reward
in your road ahead, son. Love Mom
(For Jason)

In this world of grief and woe
We follow with awe and fear
To find the place where we can go
And wipe away our tear.

It within my heart you find
Brief solitude and rest,
And, I, in your space so kind
Find comfort that is best.

On this Thanksgiving Day
I hope that we can know
The strength from God, His path, the Way
Where we can learn and grow.

In spirit and in grateful thanks
We'll sing a song of praise,
And joy will overflow the banks
Of these Thanksgiving Days.

DECEMBER SOUNDS

LoAnn Twedt © 1999

Winter comes with breath of crystal,
Blowing down upon the land.
The sound of tinkling bells ring out,
With cheerful message of God's hand.

Children sing songs of youth
That tell of Jesus birth;
When salvation came so quiet, humble
And softly stole onto the earth.

In moments after Jesus came,
Angels sang heaven's sweet song.
Joys over flowing from realms of Glory
Now to man eternally belong.

Today we hear the same sweet song,
From children blessed of God
Who see Heaven most pure and clear,
With eyes that go where angels trod.

POEMS OF FAITH

Faith is probably the most important construct one can hold. The rituals, prayers and fellowship of believers are a source of strength in times of trouble. Whatever religions you may hold to, these components are what heal people when sick, cheer them when sorrowful, and bring together a congregate fellowship of like-minded people. Strength comes in numbers.

The following poems are Christian because I hold to the Christian faith. It is so ingrained into my life that I cannot say nor do anything without it. My poems are about it. Our Christmas holiday is here because Christ was born. Call it what you like, that is the foundation of the holiday.

The poems start out as everyday poems and end with poems about Thanksgiving and Christmas. No matter what your faith, I think you can relate to these poems because we all experience what Christmas has become for us all.

TO KNOW HIM

LoAnn Twedt © 2001

To know Him is to see myself
The way He does.

To know Him is to see others
Through the eyes of compassion.

To know Him is to see His word
Through the eyes of faith.

To know Him is to see the world
With eyes of discernment.

To know Him is to see potential
In all of life circumstances.

To know Him is to call upon Him
When the way is dark and we feel lost.

To know Him is to give Him thanks
In all of life's trials for they are places of learning.

To know Him is to know that
Is how we grow in faith and character.

To know Him is to understand that the path
He has set for us is also the best way to go.

God is Love.

GROWING OLD IS NOT SUCH FUN

LoAnn Twedt © 2021

By now I know that growing old is not so very fun.
The many losses I endure make me wish I'd just begun.
When the road ahead was smooth and sure, and I was on the run.
But loss of home and loss of health
Loss of friends and loss of wealth,
Are things I wish would change.
This growing old is hard to do and sometimes, very strange.
Scripture says that's the way old age will be,
And a trip to Heaven is my only source of glee.
That's not so bad you know. It really could be worse,
I've had a long life filled with happiness and mirth.
I've been around the wheel of life, clinging on with joyous pleasure.
Waving to the crowds going by knowing life beyond all measure.
So now it's time for me to sit and watch the fun go by.
Oh, not for me or for you, we'll keep on moving on the fly.
For now, it's wisdom we impart to all the
young and middle young as well.
We've still a job and task to do until we ring our final bell.
Though, at times, life's been tough and sometimes pretty rough,
I wouldn't change a single thing I've done.
I'd like to say, "No not one."
Life is not like that either with all its griefs and sorrows,
But I'm forgiven all my goofs and will look toward to my tomorrows.

FREE WILL

LoAnn Twedt © 2003

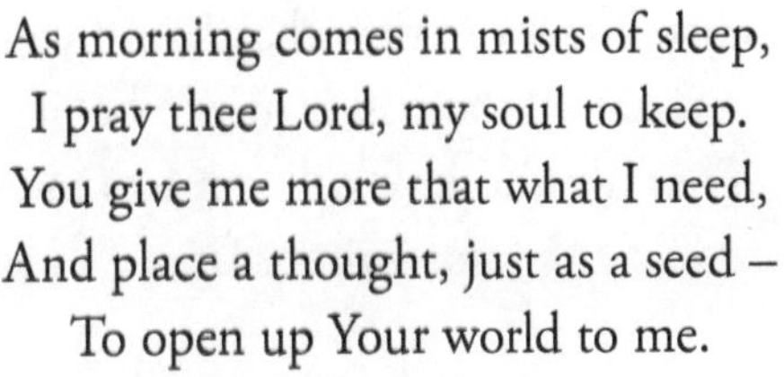

As morning comes in mists of sleep,
I pray thee Lord, my soul to keep.
You give me more that what I need,
And place a thought, just as a seed –
To open up Your world to me.

Today I see Your love for me,
In glimpses of reality.
You have a plan for me to live,
With ample praise and love to give-
To someone who is real.

But best of all, You've set me free,
From being chained to destiny.
My heart has opened one more door
That leads to acceptance, love and more-
And I can lead or follow.

IN HIS GOOD TIME

LoAnn Twedt © 1999

How sweet to know that I am free,
That all there is, is just to be,
That life and love will come to me
As Jesus will see fit.

How sweet to rest beneath His wing,
To know that in good time He'll bring
All that I need, yes, everything,
And He will not forget.

PONDERINGS

LoAnn Twedt © 1999
(For Jason)

If I could just but spread my wings
And swiftly fly to you.
I'd bring you sunshine, joy and peace,
Wrapped in a sky of blue.

This world of care invades our hearts,
And wages war within our souls,
We bend and sway, but never break
While racing to our goal.

If I could just but soar above
This world of earthly woe.
I'd take your place in sorrow's grace
And set you free to go.

Ah, but you and I are here
Till heaven's final hour
So we will pray and live each day,
With God's almighty power.

TRAVELING HOME

LoAnn Twedt © 2001

Some years ago I came this way,
To live, work, love and play.

Some years ago I longed to learn
What life's about and how to earn.

Some years ago I wished to grow
Before t'was time that I should know

Just how to take life's other side
Of life's ever flowing tide.

At times I dream, think and wonder
How many years will be the number?

What more do I have to see?
In old age, who will I be?

And then I'm gently, firmly coached
To see God's real-life approach.

From early years to now I've roamed,
And all the while was going home.

A THANKSGIVING PRAYER

LoAnn Twedt © 1999

Oh, God of mercy in this place;
We come before your throne of grace.
To give our thanks for love so kind;
And pray Your love will always find
Its way into our hearts.

Be with us all this day of thanks.
May your love over-flow the banks
To those who you, in our way, will send
Help us be kind and faithful friends
Who never more will part.

May we, through Christ, much blessing bring,
So that we make glad hearts sing,
When sharing, caring, comes from You
Given in friendship ever true.

As we do Your will today,
Remind us of the debt t'was paid
To bring this food, family, friends
Such great bounty to this end
And glory give to You.

CHRISTMAS

LoAnn Twedt © 2012

Trees and ornaments, mistletoe, holly,
Goodies and candies make Christmas jolly.
Presents and play things, shopping till dropping,
The season's activity keeps us all hopping,
With meetings and greetings and programs so fair,
That sometimes Lord Jesus just isn't there.

Without Jesus present, what's Christmas anyway?
It's just another cold, icy and wintery day.
To wrap up in blankets, bathrobes, and booties,
And while away time with obligations and duties.
Just why in the world did Jesus come to this earth?
Just why was it so very important—this birth?

Perhaps it is special because of what Jesus came for,
Forgiving and saving and opening a new door,
To heaven, a place where Christmas is always celebrated,
And love, hope and kindness are uncomplicated.
In heaven where streets are made of precious metals and gold,
And Jesus is preparing our mansions we're told.

All the shopping and presents and food can't compare,
To the gift of life that our Savior so gladly did bear.
All the family and friends, parties and programs
Are designed to keep hopping and growing money jim-jams
That will hang onto us throughout the new year
And obliterate Jesus keeping His memory austere.

So shop, play and fellowship if you must
But keep Jesus gifts of love, life and trust
In the front of your mind and the depths of your heart
And then you will true Christmas joy, love and truth impart.
All your friends, food, and programs will be especially blessed
When Jesus is honored as your number one guest.

EPILOGUE

In life we need to find activities that are fun, activities that help us learn and activities that help us grow spiritually and physically. I sincerely hope this book of poetry has done just that for you. I hope you find new places to go, new things to do and pleasure from reading the poems. This collection of poetry is a story of my life in middle age. There is nothing hidden in the pages. While imagination has to take hold when reading, know this, what you imagine and what you visualize is true. What you experience in reading is what I experienced in life.

Let the book stimulate you to be active and seek to find these activities and places. Go out and find them. It is the adventure that life is supposed to be for all of us. It will not be easy but it will certainly be enriching. Happy traveling!

www.ingramcontent.com/pod-product-compliance
Lightning Source LLC
Chambersburg PA
CBHW030428310726
48979CB00009B/1666/J

* 9 7 8 1 9 5 7 3 7 8 2 5 1 *